ANDREW LOST

12

IN THE ICE AGE

BY J. C. GREENBURG

ILLUSTRATED
BY JAN GERARDI

A STEPPING STONE BOOK™

Random House 🏠 New York

To Dan, Zack, and the real Andrew,
with a galaxy of love.
To the children who read these books: I wish
you wonderful questions. Questions are
telescopes into the universe!
—J.C.G.

To Cathy Goldsmith, with many thanks.
—J.G.

Text copyright © 2005 by J. C. Greenburg.
Illustrations copyright © 2005 by Jan Gerardi.
All rights reserved. Published in the United States by Random House
Children's Books, a division of Random House, Inc., New York.

www.randomhouse.com/kids/AndrewLost
www.AndrewLost.com

Educators and librarians, for a variety of teaching tools,
visit us at www.randomhouse.com/teachers

Library of Congress Cataloging-in-Publication Data
Greenburg, J. C. (Judith C.)
In the Ice Age / by J. C. Greenburg ; illustrated by
Jan Gerardi. — 1st ed.
    p. cm. — (Andrew Lost ; 12) "A Stepping Stone book."
SUMMARY: Still trying to stop the evil Dr. Kron-Tox, Andrew, his
cousin Judy, Thudd the robot, and Beeper find Uncle Al in the Ice
Age, where they encounter prehistoric animals, birds, and people.
ISBN 0-375-82952-0 (trade) — ISBN 0-375-92952-5 (lib. bdg.)
[1. Time travel—Fiction. 2. Glacial epoch—Fiction. 3. Prehistoric
animals—Fiction. 4. Prehistoric peoples—Fiction. 5. Cousins—Fiction.]
I. Gerardi, Jan, ill. II. Title. III. Series: Greenburg, J. C. (Judith C.).
Andrew Lost ; v 12.
PZ7.G82785Iom 2005 [Fic]—dc22 2005001110

Printed in the United States of America
First Edition 10 9 8 7 6 5 4 3 2 1

RANDOM HOUSE and colophon are registered trademarks of Random
House, Inc. ANDREW LOST is a trademark of J. C. Greenburg.

CONTENTS

ANDREW'S WORLD

Andrew Dubble

Andrew is ten years old, but he's been inventing things since he was four. Andrew's inventions usually get him into trouble, like the time he shrunk himself, his cousin Judy, and his little silver robot Thudd smaller than a fly's eye.

Today a problem with a snack has sent Andrew back in time—way back. Now he's headed for the Ice Age, trying to find his Uncle Al!

Judy Dubble

Judy is Andrew's thirteen-year-old cousin. At nine o'clock, she got into her pajamas in a cabin in Montana. A little while later, she saw the beginning of the universe, a spider the size of a desk, and a Tyrannosaurus rex!

She blames it all on Andrew.

Thudd

The Handy Ultra-Digital Detective. Thudd is a super-smart robot and Andrew's best friend. He has helped to save Andrew and Judy from an exploding star, a tsunami, and a Tyrannosaurus. But can he save them from a flood that can move mountains?

Uncle Al

Andrew and Judy's uncle is a top-secret scientist. He invented Thudd and the Time-A-Tron time-travel machine. But now he's been kidnapped and hidden in the Ice Age! Will Andrew and Judy be able to find him?

Professor Winka Wilde

She's Uncle Al's partner, and she was kidnapped, too! When Andrew and Judy found her 65 million years ago, she was stranded with a herd of triceratops!

Doctor Kron-Tox

The mysterious Doctor Kron-Tox invented a time machine, too—the Tick-Tox Box. He's used it to kidnap Uncle Al and another scientist. But why?

Beeper Jones

Andrew and Judy found nine-year-old Beeper 360 million years ago. He likes to collect dog-sized scorpions and six-foot centipedes, and—oh yes—he's Doctor Kron-Tox's nephew. Other than that, he's not a bad kid.

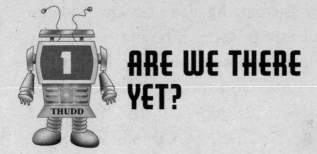

1 ARE WE THERE YET?

Why are we still stuck in dinosaur time? thought ten-year-old Andrew Dubble. He was strapped inside his uncle's time-travel vehicle, the Time-A-Tron. *Why aren't we heading for the Ice Age?*

The display on the Time-A-Tron's control panel kept blinking 65 MILLION YEARS AGO.

Sitting next to Andrew was his thirteen-year-old cousin, Judy. She was pounding the Fast-Forward button on the silvery control panel.

Outside a forest fire was roaring. Towers of flames were creeping closer.

An asteroid the size of a city had just slammed into the Earth and set off an enormous explosion. It had heated the Earth's surface to a thousand degrees and set fires all over the world.

bong . . . "The Time-A-Tron is on its side," said the Time-A-Tron in its deep, echoey voice. "One of the Fast-Fins seems to be stuck. It is not spinning."

"Hoo boy!" came a voice from the backseat. It was Beeper Jones, the boy they had rescued 300 million years ago.

Beeper was wearing just a T-shirt, underpants with pictures of penguins, and a black tube tied around his waist.

"I lost my camera," said Beeper. "I think it fell off my belt when I was getting into the Time-A-Tron. I gotta go get it. It's got the only photos of dinos in the whole world!"

"Oh no, you don't," said Professor Winka Wilde. She grabbed Beeper by the neck of his

T-shirt. They had found Professor Wilde stranded near a herd of triceratops.

"The fire will be here in seconds and the air may be too hot to breathe," said Winka.

Beeper yanked himself away. In an instant he had pulled up the door in the floor and crawled into the lower compartment.

"Beeper!" yelled Winka Wilde. "Get back here!"

"What a bozo!" yelled Judy.

"I'll get him," said Andrew, unbuckling his seat belt.

"Noop! Noop! Noop!" squeaked a voice from Andrew's pocket. It was Thudd, Andrew's little silver robot and best friend. "Big, big danger!"

bong . . . "Do not go after him, Master Andrew," said the Time-A-Tron. "I will seal the doors."

bzerk . . . bzerk . . . bzerk . . .

"The emergency escape!" said Andrew.

sssssss . . .

One of the Time-A-Tron's doors was sliding open!

bong . . . "Too late!" it groaned.

Andrew scrambled out of his chair. But just then Beeper yelled, "Found it."

bunk . . . came a sound from the bottom compartment.

"Get back here," said Winka sternly.

"Just a minute," said Beeper. "I, uh, dropped something."

bong . . . "What if we had taken off while you were outside, Master Beeper?" asked the Time-A-Tron.

"No *way*," said Beeper, crawling into the upper compartment. "Old Judy-Patootie can't even get us moving."

"Eat worms!" said Judy. "We're leaving in a second!"

"Not a chance," said Beeper. "Judy Dubble's in big, big trouble!"

"Now stop it, you two," said Winka. She was leaning over the control panel, examining the buttons. "We need to focus on getting out of here."

meep . . . "Gotta rock!" squeaked Thudd.

Judy frowned at him. "Thudd, this is *no* time for music!"

"Noop! Noop! Noop!" said Thudd. "Gotta rock Time-A-Tron. Rock side to side. Get Fast-Fin unstuck!"

"Oh!" said Judy.

"Good thinking, Thudd," said Winka.

"Let's do it!" said Beeper.

"On the count of three, rock left," said Andrew. "One . . . two . . . *three!*"

They all leaned left, then right, then back again. The Time-A-Tron rocked back and forth.

bong . . . "Good work!" said the Time-A-Tron. "Keep going!"

FLUMP!

The Fast-Fin yanked free.

WOOHOOOOOO!

Balls of green flame shot from both of the Fast-Fins. They wrapped the Time-A-Tron in a web of light.

BLAFOOOOOOOOOM!

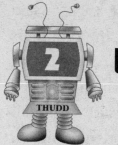

2

UH-OH . . .

The numbers on the control panel were changing!

64 MILLION YEARS AGO

63 MILLION YEARS AGO

62 MILLION YEARS AGO

bong . . . "Congratulations!" said the Time-A-Tron. "Your excellent teamwork has gotten us moving again!"

"Finally!" said Judy, leaning back in her seat.

Andrew looked out the window. The blazing fire had disappeared. There was nothing but darkness and swirling green light.

"I'm glad we got out of there," said Andrew. "But I feel awful that the dinosaurs are all going to die."

Winka sighed. "Some of them survived the fires and the heat," she said. "Animals that were in the water, or underground, or even under a pile of leaves may have lived. But then they had another big problem."

bong . . . "The asteroid blasted trillions of tons of dirt and water into the sky," said the Time-A-Tron.

meep . . . "Stuff go halfway to moon!" said Thudd.

Winka nodded. "Most of it came down again quickly. The rocks fell back to Earth as billions of meteors. But the dust circled the Earth for months."

meep . . . "Sky dark, dark, dark for long time," said Thudd. "Lotsa plants die."

bong . . . "Then the giant plant-eating dinosaurs didn't have enough to eat," said the Time-A-Tron. "And the meat-eating dinosaurs didn't have enough plant-eating dinosaurs to eat."

"Awwwwww," sighed Beeper.

bong . . . "But consider this," said the Time-A-Tron. "If huge dinosaurs did not go extinct, mammals might have stayed small, like mice and opossums."

"Or like our friend the shrew, huh?" said Judy.

bong . . . "Yes," said the Time-A-Tron. "Mammals might never have had the chance to become large, smart creatures—like you."

"Like three of us, anyway," said Beeper, pulling Judy's hair.

Winka swatted Beeper's hand away from Judy's head. Then she said, "All the dust blocking the sun made the Earth as cold as an ice age for many months."

meep . . . "Earth have lotsa ice ages," said Thudd.

Winka nodded. "It helped that mammals were warm-blooded," she said. "Warm-blooded mammals could survive the cold better than cold-blooded reptiles."

"Ice age!" said Judy. "Andrew, did you set the DNA Detector to find Uncle Al in the Ice Age?"

Andrew and Judy's uncle Al was a super-smart scientist. He had invented the Time-A-Tron and Thudd, too.

Beeper's uncle, Doctor Kron-Tox, had kid-napped Uncle Al and hidden him in Ice Age Montana. He was stranded somewhere between 20,000 and 11,000 years ago.

500,000 YEARS AGO blinked on the Time-A-Tron's display.

"Uh-oh," said Andrew. "I almost forgot."

From his pajama pocket, Andrew pulled the DNA Detector. It looked like a black remote control. He pressed the keys to spell "Alfred Dubble."

100,000 YEARS AGO
50,000 YEARS AGO
20,000 YEARS AGO

It got very quiet inside the Time-A-Tron as they waited for a signal from the DNA Detector.

15,000 YEARS AGO

14,000 YEARS AGO

ping . . . ping . . . ping . . .

The DNA Detector had detected Uncle Al!

Judy let go of the Fast-Forward button, and the web of green light around the Time-A-Tron vanished.

The time-travel machine was sitting on a rocky plain. Low plants and scruffy bushes grew between the stones. Here and there were patches of snow.

"Wowzers!" said Andrew. "Montana sure is different from when the dinosaurs lived here."

"Let's get out and look for Uncle Al," said Judy.

They unlatched their seat belts. Andrew pulled up the door in the floor and climbed down the rope ladder into the lower compartment. The others followed.

bong . . . The Time-A-Tron's oval door opened. A chilly breeze blew in.

"Woofers!" said Andrew with a shiver. "It's cold out there!"

There was a whiff of pine in the clear air, and the sky was blue and sunny.

Andrew glanced around the compartment. "I wonder if there's anything warm to wear," he said.

Hoooo . . . hoooo . . . hoooo . . .

It was the hooting of a little pygmy owl. It had chased the shrew into the Time-A-Tron before their trip.

The hoots were coming from a tangle of black fuel tubes. Andrew crawled behind the tubes.

"Holy moly!" he said, staring down at a pile of black coils. The owl was sitting on top of a huge egg! It was exactly like the Tyrannosaurus egg they had found 65 million years ago.

"Beeper!" yelled Andrew. "How did this egg get here?"

"Oh!" said Beeper. "I found it outside when I was looking for my camera."

Winka shook her head. "Beeper, bringing a Tyrannosaurus to the Ice Age is *so* wrong," she said. "We've told you before, we must not interfere with the past."

WHOOOMF! WHOOOMF! WHOOOMF!

They all turned toward the door. Something was coming. Something big!

3 A MAMMOTH PROBLEM

Something dark and furry blocked the light from the open door.

In the dimness, Andrew could see . . . a trunk! It looked like an elephant's trunk, but this one was very hairy. The trunk was attached to a dark furry face. Thick yellow tusks sprouted beneath the trunk.

meep . . . "Woolly mammoth!" squeaked Thudd.

The trunk snaked through the door and wrapped itself around Judy's waist.

"Yaaaaahhhh!" yelled Judy as the trunk began dragging her out of the Time-A-Tron.

Winka flung herself at Judy and hung on.

bong . . .

The door closed—on the mammoth's trunk!

The trunk let go of Judy and tugged itself out of the door.

"Cheese Louise!" said Judy, flopping to the floor.

Suddenly the Time-A-Tron began to totter. It was tipping!

KRUNK!

The Time-A-Tron fell on its side and started to roll. Inside the compartment, everyone was tumbling like popcorn.

"Beeper!" yelled Winka. "Grab that egg! Let's get to our seats and buckle up."

Andrew, Judy, and then Beeper with the egg made their way into the upper compartment and strapped themselves in.

"Wowzers schnauzers!" said Andrew, looking out the window. "The mammoth is *rolling* us!"

"It's like we're in a circus!" said Beeper.

"My stomach feels yucky," said Judy.

The mammoth was shoving them toward a jagged line of craggy mountains. Thudd pointed to a huge wall of ice stretched between two of the highest ones.

meep . . . "Glacier!" he said. "Moving ice mountain!"

The mammoth stopped and wagged its trunk in the air.

"It smells something," said Winka.

A creature crept out of the glacier. It looked like a heap of fur on two feet! The creature ran to the Time-A-Tron. There was pounding at the Time-A-Tron's door.

bong . . . "Who is there?" asked the Time-A-Tron.

"Ubble . . . UBBLE!" came a muffled sound.

bong . . . "Professor Dubble is here!" said the Time-A-Tron, opening the door.

They unbuckled their seat belts and rushed into the bottom compartment.

The pile of fur in the doorway seemed to bow. Fur pieces tumbled from it. Underneath the falling fur was Uncle Al, dressed like a bear.

"Hey, Uncle Al!" yelled Andrew and Judy. They scrambled into his fuzzy arms.

"Hiya, Unkie!" squeaked Thudd.

"Hello, Alfred," said Winka, smiling.

Uncle Al hugged them all.

"I *knew* Max would find you," he said
with a big smile. "And the Time-A-Tron has
taken good care of you. You all look great!"

"You don't look anything like a clown,
sir," said Beeper.

"*What?*" said Judy.

"My uncle calls *your* uncle a clown,"
explained Beeper. "But I don't think he's
right."

Uncle Al laughed. "Thank you, Beeper,"
he said. "And what would your uncle Kron-

Tox say if he saw you in your underpants holding a huge . . . egg? Beeper, don't tell me you've got a dinosaur egg there!"

Beeper grinned. "A monster fish pulled off my pants 360 million years ago," he said. "And don't worry, sir, I won't tell you about the egg."

Uncle Al shook his head. "We'll deal with that later," he said as he picked through the pile of fur. "But first we have to get you dressed for the Ice Age."

"*What?*" said Judy. "Uncle Al, now that we've found you, can't we just go back to our own time? Doctor Kron-Tox is after us. He could catch up with us any minute."

The twinkle in Uncle Al's eyes faded.

"It's not that simple," he said. He handed Judy a cape of shaggy brown fur. "There's something important we have to do first."

4 FUR-THER AND FUR-THER

"What?" asked Andrew.

Uncle Al handed Andrew a big chunk of fur. "Doctor Kron-Tox has been capturing animals from different times," he said. "He's hidden them in the glacier.

"I've found some of them, but there are more. We have to find them all and get them back to their own times. And we have to do it very fast."

"What's the rush?" asked Beeper.

"There's an enormous flood coming very soon," said Uncle Al.

"Not another stupid disaster!" said Judy.

Uncle Al held a hunk of fur up to Beeper to check the size. "The Ice Age has been getting warmer for a while now," he said.

"Not far from here, there's a huge ice dam that's two hundred stories high. It's started to melt. It could break anytime. When it does, more water than all the rivers in the world will rush out."

"Wowzers schnauzers!" said Andrew. "We've got to get Max to a safe place, too!"

"We'd better hurry," said Winka.

Winka and Uncle Al fitted everyone with capes and scarves. There were big pieces of fur to wrap around their waists like skirts. Then Uncle Al handed out small pieces of fur and leather strips.

"Here," he said. "Wrap the fur around your feet and tie it on with the leather strips. Not fashionable, but warm. Andrew, here's an extra strip. You can make a little holder for Thudd and hang him from your neck."

"Where did all this fur come from?" asked Andrew.

"I found piles of it inside the cave where I've been staying," said Uncle Al. "They're beaver skins, from giant beavers. The skins were collected by human hunters, but I haven't seen them."

Beeper wrapped his egg in a piece of fur. Then they all hopped out of the Time-A-Tron.

"Bye, Time-A-Tron!" said Andrew.

"See you soon," said Judy.

bong . . . "Keep warm!" said the Time-A-Tron.

Everyone, including Max, followed Uncle Al toward the glacier.

Andrew's breath made little clouds in the cool air. He could feel the hard, cold ground through his furry foot wraps.

"Hoo boy!" yelled Beeper, who was straggling behind. "I almost slipped on some ice. I almost dropped the egg. Can I get a ride on Max? *Please?*"

Uncle Al turned to Beeper and rolled his eyes. "Well, I guess we could arrange that," he said.

"Max!" said Uncle Al. He held his hand up. Max stopped. "Beeper, go stand in front of Max."

Uncle Al raised his hand from his waist to the top of his head.

Max curled his trunk gently around Beeper and slowly raised him to the top of his head.

"Hot doggies!" said Beeper, settling himself on top of Max's head.

Suddenly eerie sounds came from a distance.

Harooooo! Wahoooooo!

They gave Andrew the shivers.

"Wolves!" said Winka.

"Yes," said Uncle Al, looking toward a line of trees. "Two kinds of wolves live here. Dire wolves are big with small brains. They'll go extinct in a few thousand years.

"Gray wolves are smaller and smarter. The gray wolves will be alive in our time, too. Those are the ones you hear now."

Judy walked closer to Uncle Al. "That sound gives me the creeps," she said.

"They're howling to get ready to hunt," said Uncle Al. "There's no reason to fear wolves. They're not interested in hunting us.

"But if a wolf ever did attack you, you must never run. The creatures that stand and face the wolves survive."

"Even squirrels?" Beeper yelled from Max's head.

Uncle Al smiled. "It probably doesn't work for squirrels," he said.

They arrived at a jagged crack in the glacier. It was as wide as a door.

Uncle Al held up his hand to Max. He raised his other hand above his head and lowered it to his waist. Max reached his trunk up to Beeper and lowered him slowly to the ground.

Suddenly an enormous zigzag of white light slashed through the sky! They hurried into the blue shadows of the glacier entrance, then peered out to see what it was.

DOCTOR KRON-TOX!

Floating outside was an enormous cube-shaped chunk of blackness. Lightning flickered around it and inside it.

"It's the Tick-Tox Box!" said Andrew.

The Tick-Tox Box was Doctor Kron-Tox's time-travel machine.

"It looks a lot bigger now," said Judy, peering over Andrew's head.

"The Tick-Tox Box grows to fit whatever's inside it," said Uncle Al. "Doctor Kron-Tox must be carrying a big load."

The lightning inside the Tick-Tox Box faded to a flicker.

Suddenly a jagged crack split one wall of the Tick-Tox Box. Out of the crack stepped a tall, thin man in a black cape. Long white hair fell past his shoulders. His nose and mouth were covered by a white mask. In his fists he gripped fat chains.

"It's my uncle!" said Beeper, pushing in front of Uncle Al.

"Creep-a-roony!" said Judy. "Why's he wearing that stupid mask over his face?"

"He's allergic to many animals," said Winka. "He wears the mask to keep from breathing in the dander."

meep . . . "Dander is little skin flakes," said Thudd.

"Like dandruff," chuckled Beeper, pulling Judy's hair.

"Doctor Kron-Tox can't control himself when he's sneezing," said Uncle Al. "He's helpless."

Eeeeeeeeee!

From inside the Tick-Tox Box came a high-pitched scream.

Doctor Kron-Tox flung himself toward the crack in the Tick-Tox Box. He seemed to be struggling with something inside.

Andrew heard a voice that sounded like a hiss:

"Not time to go,

Not yet, I say.

Just two come now,

The rest must stay."

Doctor Kron-Tox yanked the chains. A boulder-like creature on stumpy legs crept out.

"What is *that*?" asked Judy. "It looks like a Volkswagen Bug with feet!"

"Look at that giant spiky ball at the end of its tail!" said Beeper.

meep . . . "Glyptodont!" said Thudd.

"It's a kind of giant armadillo," explained Winka.

"Doctor Kron-Tox must have stopped off in South America," said Uncle Al. "That's where those glyptodonts live."

Following slowly behind the glyptodont was a furry thing as big as an elephant. But it

GLIP-tuh-dahnt

was standing on its hind legs. It was so tall, it could look into your bedroom window, even if your bedroom was on the second floor of your house.

"Santa Claus on a snow cone!" said Uncle Al. "It's a giant ground sloth. Look how slowly it's moving."

meep . . . "Sloth mean laziness," said Thudd.

Unk . . . Unk . . . Unk . . .

Grunty noises were coming from the Tick-Tox Box.

"No! *NOOOOO!*" screamed Doctor Kron-Tox.

Suddenly a crowd of furry pig-sized animals poured out of the Tick-Tox Box.

"Hoo boy!" said Beeper, sticking his head out of the doorway. "They look like guinea pigs—*gigunda* guinea pigs!"

"In a way, they are," said Uncle Al, pulling Beeper back inside.

meep . . . "Capybara!" said Thudd.

"Right!" said Uncle Al. "Capybaras belong to the same family of animals as guinea pigs. They're rodents, like mice and rats and squirrels."

The capybaras seemed frantic to get out. They were climbing over each other. They were climbing over Doctor Kron-Tox!

"Back, back, you pigs,
Into your pen!
You brats

Will never eat again!"

The capybaras got tangled in Doctor Kron-Tox's chains.

"*AKKKK!*" he cried as he toppled over and let go of the chains.

The glyptodont scuttled down a hill and out of sight. The sloth lumbered slowly toward a pine tree.

Doctor Kron-Tox picked himself up, dusted off his cape, and yelled after the escaping animals.

"Go on, you beasts,

Do as you please.

Without my help,

You'll starve and freeze!"

Doctor Kron-Tox caught up with the sloth. He grabbed its chain and tugged the enormous animal toward the glacier. He pulled something out of a pocket and pressed it. A huge slab of ice slid aside, revealing a secret door.

6 EGGS-SPLOSION!

"I've got to go after Doctor Kron-Tox now," said Uncle Al. "He'll lead me to where he's hidden the other animals. I want you all to stay in my cave till I get back." He pointed to a path leading into the glacier. "You'll be safe and warm."

Uncle Al slipped out of the crevice and hurried after Doctor Kron-Tox.

Winka, Andrew, Judy, and Beeper made their way deeper into the glacier.

"The light is blue in here!" said Andrew.

Winka nodded. "It's like the sea," she said. "Light is made up of all the colors of the rainbow. As you go deep into water or under ice, blue is the only color that gets through. All the other colors get filtered out."

Krik . . . krik . . . krik . . .

"Hoo boy!" said Beeper. "My egg is cracking! It's gonna hatch any second! Hey, I can see its teeth!"

Judy patted Beeper on the back. "Even the little ones will try to eat you," she said.

They came to a low arch and crept under it. On the other side was a rocky cave. In the middle of the floor burned a small fire. Smoke curled up to a crack in the ceiling.

"It's cozy here," said Judy. She squinted at the walls. "Look at this," she said, tracing her fingers along the dark stone.

The walls were covered with drawings!

"Neato mosquito!" said Andrew. "I found a herd of galloping horses!"

Winka pointed out long-horned bison drawn in brown and black.

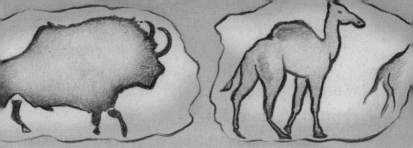

"Hey!" said Beeper. "I see a camel!"

Winka came over to look. "Yes," she said. "Camels lived in North America during the Ice Age. Look, there's the beginning of another animal here, but the artist didn't finish it."

Winka leaned down to examine a stone bowl on the floor. "I've found the artist's tools!" she said.

She held up fat sticks of black and red and brown.

"The black one is charcoal," said Winka. "The red and brown ones are made from a mineral called hematite. Hematite has lots of iron in it."

"Here's a really strange picture," said Judy. "I can't figure it out."

Winka came over to see it. It looked like two mountains. Between them was a white wall with a zigzag crack. Giant waves were painted all around it.

"That must be the ice dam your uncle Al told us about," said Winka.

"Ouch!" yelled Beeper. "The Tyrannosaurus nipped my neck!"

He held the cracked egg as far away from himself as he could.

Winka hurried to a heap of fur scraps in a dark nook. "We need to wrap up that little guy to keep both of you safe," said Winka.

KREEEEEEEEEK!

The cave trembled and the fire flickered. The baby Tyrannosaurus kicked off its broken egg and scrambled into Beeper's arms.

meep . . . "Sound of glacier ice cracking," said Thudd. "Ice crack. Ice move. Glacier noisy."

KREEEEEEEEEEEEEEEEK!

The cave shook again. Bits of rock fell from the ceiling.

KREEEEEEEEEEEEEEEK!

"Down, boy!" said Beeper to the Tyrannosaurus baby.

The Tyrannosaurus sank its teeth into
Beeper's cape, leapt out of his arms, and scam-
pered out of the cave.

"I'll get it!" said Winka, chasing after the
little dinosaur. "You stay here till I get back."

Judy rolled her eyes at Beeper. "Nice work,
Bozo-Boy," she said.

Beeper picked up one of the colored
sticks. In big letters on the cave wall, he wrote

"I LOVE DINOSAURS!" Then he drew the head of a Tyrannosaurus.

"I'm worried about those capybaras," said Andrew, pacing the stone floor. "It's too cold for them outside. Maybe we could find them. Then we could bring them back here where it's warm."

"They were pretty cute," said Judy. Her eyes had a faraway look. "They reminded me of my guinea pig, Nibbles."

"I remember Nibbles," said Andrew. "He liked to eat my shirt."

meep . . . "Not supposed to leave cave," squeaked Thudd.

Beeper stopped drawing. Andrew, Judy, and Beeper looked at each other.

"Uncle Al and Professor Winka wouldn't want the capybaras to freeze," said Andrew.

"For once I agree with you, Bug-Brain," said Judy.

"Hookay!" said Beeper. "Let's go!"

ON THE TRAIL OF THE GIANT GUINEA PIGS

"Wait a minute," said Judy. "We'd better leave a note."

She grabbed a reddish drawing stick. On the wall she wrote: "Gone to save the capybaras. Be back soon."

She reached under her fur cape and pushed the stick into her pocket. Then they crept onto the cool blue path through the glacier.

When they arrived at the glacier's entrance, Andrew poked his head out.

The Tick-Tox Box was still there. It was dark now, and it had shrunk to the size of Andrew's bedroom closet.

From the glacier to the faraway trees, nothing was moving but Max. He plodded over to them with his ears spread wide.

meep . . . "Max say 'Hello' with ears," said Thudd.

Beeper stuck his thumbs in his ears and wiggled his fingers at Max.

Max touched Beeper with the tip of his trunk. He seemed to be sniffing him.

"Elephants have a gigunda sense of smell," said Beeper. "Once a herd of elephants smelled my uncle from a mile away. They stampeded!"

meep . . . "Elephant may be best smeller on Earth," said Thudd. "Mammoth is great smeller, too. That how Max find Drewd and Oody. Drewd and Oody related to Unkie Al. Smell kinda like him."

"Wowzers schnauzers!" said Andrew. "If Max tracked us, maybe he can track the capybaras!"

"Wait a minute," said Judy. "When you want a dog to track a person, you have to let the dog sniff something that has the person's smell."

meep . . . "Like stinky sock," said Thudd.

"Hoo boy!" said Beeper. "That's why Max found you guys so fast. You haven't had a bath since the beginning of the universe!"

Judy rolled her eyes. "Well, you don't exactly smell like a rose," she said. "*You* haven't had a bath in *three hundred million years!*"

Andrew was looking at a patch of trampled snow. "I think these are capybara footprints," he said.

"Yoop! Yoop! Yoop!" said Thudd.

Andrew followed the footprints to a sheet of bare rock. He couldn't find a trail.

"If we could get Max to sniff these foot-prints," said Andrew, "maybe he could follow the trail of the capybaras."

"Hooey!" said Beeper. He gathered a

handful of grass and held it near the mammoth's trunk.

Max reached out his trunk. With two little flaps at the end of it, he picked a single stem of grass. He curled his trunk toward his mouth and chewed.

Beeper wagged the rest of the grass at Max, then spread the grass over the capybara footprints. After Max gathered up every stem, he sniffed the footprints. After a moment, he started following them!

"Hey! Wait a minute!" yelled Andrew.

He ran up to Max, stood between his enormous tusks, and held up his hand. Then Andrew raised his other hand from his waist to the top of his head.

Max touched Andrew's chest with his trunk, then slowly wrapped his trunk around Andrew's waist.

It's like being hugged by a hairy snake, thought Andrew.

Max lifted Andrew to the top of his head. Andrew grabbed Max's hair and pulled himself onto the mammoth's back.

Max's hair was longer than Judy's hair. It was longer than Andrew's arm!

"Come on up, guys!" said Andrew, scooting backward. "We can all fit up here."

"Yahoo!" said Beeper.

Max scooped him up, too. Judy was next.

"This is *not* comfortable," said Judy, settling herself in front of Beeper.

"Poor Judy Patootie!" said Beeper. "They don't make saddles for *mammoths*!"

"Stuff a sock in it, Beeper Creeper!" said Judy.

The mammoth wagged its trunk across the footprints and lurched ahead. Andrew, Judy, and Beeper swayed with every step. The mammoth crossed a rocky field and crunched through patches of ice.

Sunlight glinted off the snowy ground.

Under Andrew's cloak, his arms tingled with goose bumps.

"I liked Montana better sixty-five million years ago," said Andrew.

"Yeah!" said Beeper. "When there were Tyrannosauruses."

"The Tyrannosauruses were good," said

Andrew, "but I liked that it was warm, like a jungle. I wonder why it got so cold."

meep . . . "Earth have lotsa ice ages," said Thudd. "Lotsa reasons. One reason is cuz Earth make different kindsa orbits around sun." Thudd pointed to his face screen. "When orbit like circle, Earth warm. When orbit like

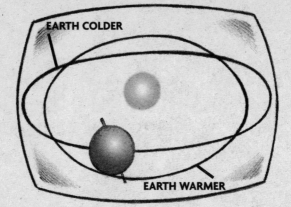

oval, Earth go farther from sun. Earth get cold. Ice not melt. Pile up. Make lotsa glaciers. Animals change. Plants change."

Harooooo! Haroooooo!

The wolves were howling somewhere out of sight.

Max plodded down a steep valley and into a pine forest. The spiky branches snapped in the kids' faces, and snow fluttered down from the treetops.

Andrew could hear the sound of water splashing. He heard another sound, too.

Unk . . . Unk . . . Unk . . .

"It's the capybaras!" Judy cried.

LIONS AND TIGERS AND TERATORNS!

Judy pointed to a clearing ahead.

A wide stream flowed from the bottom of a huge wall of ice. The ice wall was wedged into a rock canyon.

meep . . . "Ice dam!" said Thudd. "Ice dam melting! Make stream!"

Capybaras were drinking from the stream. Some were pawing the snow and nibbling bushes.

"Cheese Louise!" said Judy. "This is what Uncle Al warned us about! Let's get these giant guinea pigs moving and get out of here—*fast!*"

Skeeeek! Skeeeek!

The sound came from the sky.

"What's that?" asked Beeper. They all looked up.

High above the clearing, gigantic birds were circling.

meep . . . "Teratorn bird," said Thudd. "Biggest bird that ever fly. Long as two cars from tip of wing to tip of wing. Teratorn weigh more than Uncle Al."

Two of the teratorn birds swooped down. The capybaras scattered.

"We've got to round them up," said Andrew.

"We'll be kinda like cowboys," said Beeper.

Judy rolled her eyes. "More like *guinea pig* boys," she said.

"Let's get down off of Max," said Andrew. "Judy, you first."

"Great," said Judy, creeping to the top of Max's head.

Max understood. He wrapped his trunk

around Judy's waist and gently lowered her down.

Beeper and Andrew followed.

"We'll get behind the capys," said Andrew, "one of us on each side."

AGGGRRRRAAAAAGHHH!

A thunderous roar echoed off the canyon cliffs.

From the corner of his eye, Andrew caught a flash of tan on a ledge of the canyon.

"Yikes!" screamed Judy, catching sight of it, too.

Crouched in the rocks was a giant cat with two huge curving teeth.

meep . . . "Saber-toothed tiger!" said Thudd.

AGGGRRRRAAAAAGHHH!

Suddenly two more cats sprang down from a higher ledge. These cats were even bigger than the saber-toothed tiger, but without the gigantic teeth.

meep . . . "Lions!" squeaked Thudd.

"Hoo boy!" said Beeper. "I didn't know there were lions in America!"

Judy shivered. "I've seen lions in Africa, but these are bigger! We can't run, because they're faster than we are. We can't even turn our backs on them. Turning your back on a lion or a tiger says, 'Eat me!'"

They all stood very still and kept their eyes on the cats.

The big cats crouched and flicked their tails. They were watching, too.

The teratorns were circling high in the sky.

"How about if we jump into the stream?" said Beeper. "Cats hate water."

Judy shook her head. "Tigers *love* to swim," she said. "Maybe these cats do, too. Do you know, Thudd?"

meep . . . "Nobody know," said Thudd.

"I've got an idea," said Andrew. "Let's throw some of the fur stuff we're wearing at the cats. Maybe that will keep them busy while we escape."

Judy patted Andrew's shoulder. "It's your idea," said Judy. "So you get to take off *your* warm, furry stuff."

Andrew unwrapped the fur scarf around his neck and handed it to Judy.

"You're the best at throwing," he said.

Judy dangled the piece between her fingers. "Look at the size of those cats," she said. "They won't even notice this."

Andrew took off the big piece of fur wrapped around his waist.

Judy nodded. "That's more like it," she said.

"You can have this, too," said Beeper, handing Judy a long, ragged strip of fur. "I'd rather be cold than chewed."

The cats were watching them. Their growls rumbled through the chilly air. The teratorns swooped lower.

Judy wrapped the fur into a ball and threw it toward the cats. It landed on a ledge below the snarling animals. They jumped down and pounced on it.

Judy ripped a big chunk of fur into small

pieces and tossed them on the ground.

The teratorns began to swoop down and snatch them up.

"Woofers!" said Andrew. "Let's round up these giant guinea pigs and go!"

Andrew, Judy, and Beeper got behind the herd of capybaras and started yelling.

"Head 'em up!" hollered Andrew. "Move 'em out!"

"Giddy up, li'l dogies!" yelled Beeper.

"Shoo! *Shooo!*" yelled Judy.

Unk . . . Unk . . . Unk . . .

The furry brown animals circled around each other. They began trekking into the woods.

Max followed behind.

KREEEEEEEEEK! echoed a huge sound through the forest.

meep . . . "Ice dam cracking!" squeaked Thudd.

PLEASE DON'T EAT US! WE TASTE *TERRIBLE*!

They all turned to look.

At the top of the ice wall was a zigzag crack.

"Yowzers!" said Andrew. "It's like the cave painting."

Judy turned to Thudd. "Does this mean we'll get washed away in another fifteen seconds?" she asked.

meep . . . "Not know," said Thudd. "Flood happen anytime."

"Then let's move it!" said Judy.

In the shadows ahead, Andrew glimpsed a dark lump.

It looked like a boulder, but it was rocking and squirming. And it was noisy!

Nyeeek! Nyeeek!

"What's that?" asked Andrew.

Beeper ran up to it. "It's the glyptodont! It's on its back!"

"Uh-oh," said Andrew. "It's awfully heavy. I don't know how we can get it back on its feet."

Max went up to the glyptodont and touched it with his trunk. The glyptodont rocked from side to side and wiggled its armored feet in the air.

Max shoved his enormous tusks beneath the squirming glyptodont and scooped it up!

Nyeeek! Nyeeek! the glyptodont screeched. It didn't know it was being rescued.

"Wowzers schnauzers!" said Andrew.

"Way to go, Max!" shouted Beeper.

"*Good* mammoth!" said Judy.

They left the forest and started climbing

through snow and over rocks. They were scrambling higher and higher toward the glacier.

The capybaras grunted, but they kept together and hurried along.

"Whew!" said Andrew. "I'm getting pretty warm." He loosened the cape around his shoulders.

"I'm getting tired," complained Judy.

"Maybe I could take one of the capybaras back to our time," said Beeper. "I mean, they're just big guinea pigs."

Judy rolled her eyes. "Don't even think about it," she said.

Beeper stuck his tongue out at Judy and made a rude sound.

meep . . . "Capybaras alive in our time, too," said Thudd. "Beeper can find capybara when we get back."

"*If* we get back," said Judy.

Andrew glimpsed a long dark shape lying

on the snow. It looked familiar, but it was too big to be . . .

"A feather!" said Andrew, stopping to examine it. The feather was longer than Andrew and as wide as his foot.

meep . . . "Teratorn feather!" said Thudd.

"Andrew!" yelled Judy. "Get back here! The capys are getting away!"

Andrew picked up the feather and ran back to his side of the herd.

"Hot doggies!" said Beeper. "What a great feather! Can I have it?"

"Maybe we can share it," said Andrew.

Judy squinted at a rocky ridge ahead.

"I saw something move," she said.

"Where?" asked Andrew.

"There," said Judy, pointing.

A shadowy figure walked out from behind the ridge.

"It's a person!" Judy cried.

"It's not Professor Winka," said Andrew.

meep . . . "Not Unkie Al," said Thudd.

"It's not my uncle, either," said Beeper.

One by one, others joined the first figure. There were five of them. In single file, they walked slowly closer.

meep . . . "Ice Age people!" said Thudd.

"They're carrying *spears*!" said Judy.

meep . . . "Ice Age people hunt mammoth," said Thudd.

"Holy moly!" said Andrew, looking at Max and the little herd of capybaras. "These guys must look like lunch!"

"What if they're *cannibals*?" asked Judy.

"We'll tell them that girls taste better than boys," said Beeper.

Judy poked Beeper. "Shhhhh!" she hushed. "They're almost here."

The Ice Age people stopped in front of them. There were three men and two boys. Their black hair was long and straight and hung down their backs. They wore fur jackets,

leather pants, and hairy boots. Each one carried a spear.

"Kah mika," said the tallest man, looking at Andrew.

Andrew shrugged his shoulders. "I'm sorry," he said. "I don't understand what you're saying."

"Iktal okook!" said one of the hunters. He gestured toward Max with the tip of his spear.

"Oh, *please* don't eat Max!" pleaded Andrew. He pointed to Max and shook his head.

The hunters aimed their spears and slowly surrounded them.

10 STRANGE STRANGERS

"No! No!" shouted Andrew.

"Don't shout," said Judy softly. "You don't want them to think you're angry. We want to show them we're friendly. Maybe if we gave them a gift or something . . ."

"What do we have that's not a mammoth or a glyptodont or a giant guinea pig?" asked Andrew.

"What about the feather?" asked Judy. "It's a pretty amazing feather."

"I wanna keep it," said Beeper.

"Would you rather have the feather or your skin?" asked Judy.

Beeper shrugged.

Andrew held out the enormous feather and walked up to the hunter who'd spoken to him.

"I have something for you, sir," he said.

The man pushed the point of his spear into the ground. Then he took the feather, put his hand on Andrew's shoulder, and nodded.

One of the boys came over and touched the feather.

"Hyas chak-chak tupso," he said.

The other boy, just a little taller than Andrew, pointed to Thudd.

"Thudd," said Andrew. He held Thudd up.

"Thudd!" said the boy, smiling.

meep . . . "Hiya!" said Thudd. The boy touched Thudd's face screen. Thudd wiggled his antennas.

The boy laughed. He held out his spear to Andrew.

"Thank you," said Andrew. He took the

spear. It had a sharp point made of carved stone.

Andrew smiled and nodded. The boy smiled and nodded, too.

The tallest hunter waved his hand toward the distance.

"He's telling us to go," said Andrew.

"These guys were heading toward the ice dam," said Judy. "It could break soon. We have to warn them."

"How?" asked Andrew.

Judy stepped forward, pointed toward the dam, and shook her head.

They stared at Judy and shook their heads, too.

Beeper pointed in the direction of the dam and yelled, "BOOM!"

The hunters laughed.

"Wait a minute," said Judy.

She reached into a pajama pocket and pulled out the reddish stick she had taken from the cave.

She brushed snow off a flat rock and started to draw. The hunters gathered around her. She drew the wall with the zigzag crack that she had seen in the cave painting. She drew big waves around it.

The hunters' eyes lit up. They nodded. They recognized the drawing!

One of the hunters touched the colored stick in Judy's hand. She gave it to him. He broke it in half and gave one half to Judy.

He went up to Max and waved to Judy. He wanted her to come, too.

Nyeeek! Nyeeek! Nyeeek!

The glyptodont was frantic about having people so close.

The hunter began to rub the red color over one of Max's tusks. He motioned Judy to color the other tusk.

Soon they were done. The hunter pointed to his spear, then he pointed to Max and shook his head.

"He's telling us that they've marked Max

so they'll never hunt him!" said Andrew.

Judy, Andrew, and Beeper smiled and nodded.

The hunters did the same. Then they turned and hurried off in the direction they had come from.

Max lurched forward with a wriggling glyptodont in his tusks. The capys decided to munch some grass. Judy broke a twig off a bush and poked their behinds to hurry them along.

It wasn't long before they glimpsed the craggy ice of the glacier.

The Tick-Tox Box was where it had been when they left. But now it was bigger than a football field!

Next to it was the Time-A-Tron. It was floating a few feet off the ground and its Fast-Fins were spinning.

They were getting close to the glacier when suddenly they heard screaming. It was coming from inside the glacier, and it was getting louder.

"What's *that*?" asked Judy.

Suddenly Doctor Kron-Tox rushed out of an icy crack in the glacier wall.

"It's my uncle!" said Beeper.

Right behind him was a very tall creature that looked kind of like a dinosaur.

meep . . . "Titanis bird!" said Thudd. "Called terror bird! Ten feet tall! Fierce hunter bird! Beak bite through bone!"

Doctor Kron-Tox was running so fast that his black cape fluttered like wings. But the

Titanis bird was right behind him. And catching up with them was furry Uncle Al!

Doctor Kron-Tox was racing toward the Tick-Tox Box.

"We've got to help Uncle Al," said Andrew. "We can't let Doctor Kron-Tox get away."

"Let's block the path to the Tick-Tox Box," said Judy.

She swatted the behinds of the capys. They grunted and scrambled along.

Nyeeek! Nyeeek! Nyeeek! the glyptodont squealed as Max picked up speed.

They reached the Tick-Tox Box just in time. Doctor Kron-Tox's path was blocked by the capybaras. He shook with fury and screamed.

"Get out, go away,
You little blokes!
I'm leaving now,
This is no joke!"

"He's still wearing that stupid mask," said Judy. "I wonder what would happen if . . ."

BACK TO THE FUTURE!

Judy darted behind Doctor Kron-Tox and poked her twig at the back of his head. The twig caught the elastic that held his mask. She pulled it off Doctor Kron-Tox's face!

His eyes grew huge and round. His thin lips opened wide and trembled.

ah ah AHCHOOOOOOOO!

Doctor Kron-Tox's tall body folded like a beach chair and flopped to the ground.

AH AH AHCHOOOOOOOOOOOOOO!

He sneezed and sneezed. One of the capybaras began to lick him!

Meanwhile, the Titanis bird was jabbing

its beak at one of the capybaras.

Max, still stuck with the angry glyptodont, somehow managed to fling his trunk around the bird's neck.

Uncle Al rushed to where Doctor Kron-Tox lay helplessly sneezing.

"Rudolph the red-nosed reindeer on rye toast!" exclaimed Uncle Al with a big smile. "You guys are amazing!"

"Uncle Al!" said Judy. "The ice dam is cracking! We saw it!"

"We have to hurry," said Uncle Al. "But we must never panic. Panic makes brains freeze."

Uncle Al leaned over the sneezing Doctor Kron-Tox, pulled his arms behind his back, and tied his wrists with a strip of leather.

"Ah, my old friend," sighed Uncle Al, "you've created a bundle of problems."

Doctor Kron-Tox hissed back,

"You can't stop me
Or hold me down.

I'll have my way,

You foolish clown!"

AHCHOOOOOOOOOOOOOO!

"Gesundheit!" said Uncle Al. "You and I are going on a little trip in time and space. We're going to return all the creatures you've interfered with."

Uncle Al pulled Doctor Kron-Tox onto his feet and guided him into the Tick-Tox Box.

KYAAAAAAACK! KYAAAAAAACK!

The screaming Titanis bird was making the capybaras frantic.

"Get the capys into the Tick-Tox Box," said Uncle Al. "Get Max inside, too. We'll take him to higher ground."

Inside the dark, flickering space were many pens filled with animals. Roaring, screeching sounds came from all directions.

Haroooooo! Haroooooooo!

The wolves were somewhere inside the Tick-Tox Box. They, too, would go to high ground.

The kids found an empty pen and shooed the giant guinea pigs into it.

Max stood in the middle of the space, carrying the glyptodont and holding the Titanis bird. There wasn't another empty pen.

Andrew raised his hand to Max. "Max, you have to stay here," he said. "Uncle Al will bring you to a safe place."

Max's eyes were shiny in the darkness. Andrew waved good-bye. Beeper stuck his thumbs in his ears and wiggled his fingers. Judy blew Max a kiss. Thudd wiggled his antennas.

As the kids were coming out of the Tick-Tox Box, a familiar voice greeted them.

"You're back!" called Winka.

She was carrying the little Tyrannosaurus. But now it was wearing a muzzle made of leather strips.

"Hot doggies!" said Beeper, patting the dinosaur on the head. "How did you get him back?"

"I caught up with him when he tried to attack a giant beaver," said Winka. "The beaver was the size of a grizzly bear. It wasn't pretty."

Uncle Al guided Andrew, Judy, and Beeper toward the Time-A-Tron.

"I've loaded all Doctor Kron-Tox's captured animals into the Tick-Tox Box," said Uncle Al.

"I also checked out the Time-A-Tron. It's working perfectly now, and there's enough fuel for your trip back to our time.

"Winka and I will use the Tick-Tox Box to take all the animals back where they belong."

bong . . . "Welcome, children!" said the Time-A-Tron. "We are going home!"

"Can't we go with *you,* Uncle Al?" pleaded Andrew.

"Yeah!" said Beeper. "I'll take care of my Tyrannosaurus!"

Uncle Al smiled and shook his head. "I'm sorry," he said. "The Tick-Tox Box is a very strange vehicle and our job is too dangerous.

Besides, your parents must be worried about you."

"Naah," said Beeper. "They like me to go away as much as possible."

"Good luck, Uncle Al," said Andrew.

Judy gave Uncle Al a hug. Beeper made a rude sound.

They climbed into the bottom compartment of the Time-A-Tron.

Hooooo . . . hooooo . . . The little owl greeted them from the top of the fuel tank.

As they were climbing into the top compartment, Andrew heard a sound like distant thunder.

KRAAAAAAAAAAAAAAAAK!

They rushed to their seats.

"Cheese Louise," said Judy. "Look!"

Through the dome of the Time-A-Tron, Andrew saw a towering wall of water that seemed to reach the sky. It was carrying trees. It was carrying boulders the size of department stores. It was rushing toward them!

bong . . . "Hurry, Mistress Judy," said the Time-A-Tron. "Press the Fast-Forward button."

meep . . . "Fast! Fast! Fast!" said Thudd.

Judy slammed the Fast-Forward button with her fist.

WOOOHOOOOOOO!

Fiery green balls flew off the Fast-Fins. Through the twisting ribbons of light, they could see the Tick-Tox Box. Three gigantic bolts of white lightning zigzagged from inside it and sizzled toward the sky. Just as the humongous wave was about to smash over the Tick-Tox Box, it disappeared!

bong . . . "Professor Dubble and Winka are safely off!" said the Time-A-Tron.

Now the gigantic wave was crashing over the Time-A-Tron. It shook as the black water smashed enormous rocks and chunks of forest against the dome!

Judy slammed the Fast-Forward button once more.

BLAFOOOOOOOM!

A cocoon of green light spun around the Time-A-Tron.

13,000 YEARS AGO, read the display on the control panel.

12,000 YEARS AGO

11,000 YEARS AGO

"Whew!" said Judy. "I can't believe it!"

bong . . . "We'll be back in modern Montana in a few seconds!" said the Time-A-Tron.

"Hooey!" shouted Beeper.

Yikes! thought Andrew. *Mrs. Carmody asked me to think up a super-duper project for the school science contest. Something about how to help the environment and win a thousand dollars for poor kids in Mexico. I can't believe I forgot all about it! Wait a minute. Garbage . . . garbage . . . I've got it. A new way to get rid of garbage! YES!!! The Goa Constrictor!*

TO BE CONTINUED IN ANDREW, JUDY, AND THUDD'S

NEXT EXCITING ADVENTURE:

ANDREW LOST IN THE GARBAGE!

In stores January 2006

TRUE STUFF

Thudd wanted to tell you more about the Ice Age, but he was busy helping Andrew and Judy get back to their own time. Here's what he wanted to say:

• When living things die, bacteria eat them. So do molds and funguses. This makes dead things rotten and stinky. And after a while, they turn into dust.

But in special conditions, the hard parts of animals, like bones, absorb minerals in the soil and become hard as stone. We say they have become fossilized. We know most extinct animals only by their fossilized skeletons.

But in some very cold places, people have

found mammoths that have been frozen for thousands of years. Yet they look as though they died just a few days ago.

That's because very low temperatures keep bacteria and molds and funguses from growing. That's why the food in your freezer lasts much longer than food you keep on your kitchen counter or in your refrigerator.

If you didn't put raw meat into the refrigerator, it would be unsafe to eat in just a few hours. In a day or so, it would get very stinky. But if you wrap the meat up and store it in the freezer, it can last for months.

You can do an experiment. Take three slices of bread. Put each one in a plastic bag and seal it. Keep one slice on your kitchen counter or in your classroom, put one slice in a refrigerator, and put one slice in a freezer.

Check the slices every day and make notes. What does each slice of bread look like after one week, two weeks, three weeks?

You can't see the bacteria that are eating the bread, but you can see mold, the green or black fuzzy stuff.

It may seem yucky, but we should say a little thank-you to bacteria and molds and funguses. Without these little guys, the Earth would be piled hundreds of miles high with the bodies of dead things. Fortunately, these tiny creatures turn things like dinosaurs and tulips into molecules that go back into the soil to make other living things, such as roses, tomatoes, ladybugs, pandas, kangaroos, whales—and you!

• Some people think we could breed new mammoths from the frozen mammoths we've discovered. To do that, we would need to find a special molecule called DNA inside the cells of the mammoths.

DNA molecules are information molecules. They give instructions about what living things look like and how they work. A goldfish looks like a goldfish and acts like a gold-fish because it has goldfish DNA molecules. It's true for giraffes and gorillas, too.

Each and every human (except identical twins) has different DNA molecules. Do people tell you that you look like your mom or your dad? Maybe your eyes are blue like your dad's and maybe you've got red hair like your mom. That's because of the DNA molecules you got from both of them before you were born.

DNA molecules are long and they fall apart after an animal dies. We don't know how to use the broken DNA molecules from dead mammoths to breed living mammoths—yet. But maybe someday someone will discover a way to do it. Maybe *you* will!

WHERE TO FIND MORE TRUE STUFF

- *Ice Age Mammals of North America: A Guide to the BIG, the HAIRY, and the BIZARRE* by Ian M. Lange (Missoula, MT: Mountain Press Publishing Company, 2002).
- *Beyond the Dinosaurs! Sky Dragons, Sea Monsters, Mega-Mammals, and Other Prehistoric Beasts* by Howard Zimmerman (New York: Atheneum, 2001). Not every bizarre creature that lived millions of years ago was a dinosaur!
- *Sunset of the Sabertooth* by Mary Pope Osborne (New York: Random House Books for Young Readers, 1996). You'll be holding your breath as Jack and Annie encounter cave bears, woolly mammoths, sabertooth cats—and Ice Age humans!
- *Sabertooths and the Ice Age* by Mary Pope

Osborne and Natalie Pope Boyce (New York: Random House Books for Young Readers, 2005). Discover the facts behind the fiction in this non-fiction companion to *Sunset of the Sabertooth*.

• *Ice Age Mammoth: Will This Ancient Giant Come Back to Life?* by Barbara Hehner (New York: Crown, 2001).

• *Ice Age Sabertooth: The Most Ferocious Cat That Ever Lived* by Barbara Hehner (New York: Crown, 2003). Both of these books will drag you kicking and screaming into the Ice Age. Be sure to wear something warm!

Turn the page
for a sneak peek at
Andrew, Judy, and Thudd's
next exciting adventure—

ANDREW LOST
IN THE GARBAGE!

Available January 2006

1 SSSSSSS . . .

"Yerrrrghhh!" groaned ten-year-old Andrew Dubble. He was dragging a heavy black bag through his classroom door. The bag was squirming!

No one else was in the room.

"Wowzers!" said Andrew. "We've finally got the place to ourselves."

Ch . . . ch . . . ch . . . ch . . . ch!

Angry screams were coming from a cage behind Andrew. It was Harry and Howard, the class guinea pigs.

Andrew felt a poke inside his shirt pocket.

meep . . . "Animals afraid, Drewd," came a squeaky voice.

It was Andrew's little silver robot and best

friend, Thudd. Thudd was short for The Handy Ultra-Digital Detective.

Andrew looked around the room. A forest of trees reached for the ceiling. Plants with giant leaves pressed against the windows. Plastic hamster trails zigzagged through it all.

A shelf at the back held roomy cages for mice and guinea pigs. A hairy tarantula spider the size of Andrew's hand lived in a sandy aquarium.

"Don't worry, Thudd," said Andrew. "I'll make sure the Goa Constrictor eats just the garbage."

Andrew checked the clock on the wall. "The cafeteria ladies said they would bring the garbage at three o'clock," he said. "We've got fifteen minutes to get ready."

Andrew untied the squirming black bag and pulled a small remote control from his pants pocket. He pressed the Slither Out button.

Sssssssssssss . . . came a loud hiss from the bag. A giant brown snake head poked out. It had blinking red lights for eyes. A thin black tongue flicked from its mouth.

Its brown and yellow body slithered slowly out. It was as thick as a wastebasket and as long as a ladder.

Andrew beamed. "Wowzers schnauzers! Isn't the Goa *beautiful*?"

"Yoop! Yoop! Yoop!" said Thudd. "But gotta be careful, Drewd. Remember Atom Sucker."

Not long ago, Andrew had invented the Atom Sucker. It shrunk things by sucking the empty space out of atoms.

Andrew accidentally shrunk himself so small that he got snuffled into the nose of a dog, flushed down a toilet, and almost eaten by a nasty neighbor.

Andrew laughed. "I'll never forget *that*," he said.

"Andrew!" came a voice from the hall. It was Judy, Andrew's thirteen-year-old cousin!